GLASS/FIRE

Glass/Fire

Mandira Pattnaik

Querencia Press – Chicago IL

QUERENCIA PRESS

© Copyright 2024
Mandira Pattnaik

All Rights Reserved

No reproduction, copy or transmission of this publication may be made
without written permission.
No paragraph of this publication may be reproduced, copied, or transmitted
save with the written permission of the author.

Any person who commits any unauthorized act in relation to this publication
may be liable to criminal prosecution and civil claims for damages.

ISBN 978 1 963943 13 9

www.querenciapress.com

First Published in 2024

Querencia Press, LLC
Chicago IL

Printed & Bound in the United States of America

Glass/Fire is dedicated to all the girls of underprivileged background who must make the best of their circumstances in order to survive.

CONTENTS

Glass/Fire 11

Un~broken 13

Someone Like Annabelle 16

We Stay As You Left Us 18

Close as Breath 19

Lambda 22

Carbon is a Stranded Stone 25

Stitches 28

Tide 31

A Harvest Mismatch 34

Rodent Behavior 37

Porcellanidae 40

On the Sunday Before He leaves, Lily is the Lighthouse 42

Jamun 44

Introductory Flying Lesson 45

Churchyard Kurseong 48

A German Reunion 51

Unknot 53

Half-kissed Girlfriend 56

Prosody of Rains 60

Cullet 62

Do You Know About The Funny Parcel That Got Returned 64

Gift 66

Asking To Be Married To A Dress 67

In a Room — A Chandelier Aglow 69

Notes on Previous Publications 73

Glass/Fire

In the mood we were in, fire could be liquid, could be sand, or molten like lava, or flames, licking the last of us. Inching closer, Annabelle, red as henna, as cinnamon, as coals in the oven, the color of syrup, asked if *until evening* was too long. The two boys at the end of the room, remained huddled like uprooted weeds. *Do you know the song, Aye dil hai muskil...?* said the girl I no longer remember the name of. I could hear the boys mumbling something in answer, their teeth chattering. We girls, just about sixteen, felt the strange power of something beautiful, the way flames are—vivid, delectable, ochre—but also limitless, something that could singe you, burn you. One of the boys began coughing. The man from Alimuddin's Indian Kitchen, raw as vengeance, rough as the bark of hound dogs up in Alaska, who had come to our aid, smiled silly. He stretched his hand and pulled the curtain like he perhaps did when he dressed and left for work. The restaurant was closed for something or the other. Annabelle read the notice on the side wall like she would regard the violets by her bedside, with the same teasing flourish she displayed to the boys earlier, as we walked down from school. The same vaunt of beauty that would be dead by the time the marriage-for-citizenship the man would trick her into many weeks later—bearing the strain of an indigo ocean, the fault-lines of impermanent earth—would end. At this moment in time though, now, the helplessness of the boys, their combustible masses, same as haystack waiting for a flicker, enthralled us. We

laughed how the boys, our classmates, cold in their undies, had
to hold their pee because they were, for once, caught spying on
us. Only much later, in our Physics class, we'd know it takes
nearly the same temperature to make glass from sand as the heat
of atomic explosion. And still later, how that day had enough
ammunition to break one of the boys, shatter him like glass.

Un~broken

We're forever outsiders. Forever lonely. We chip off, we shatter. We scatter like Bone China, dropped.

We're never quite the same. However much the cracks are glued.

Breaking isn't always *into*, but *away*.

In the years since we've been here—outsiders, workers—it'd have been possible to grow immune to breaking every day. Like I am to the daily shout-fests between my parents. But I still wash okras and chilies and finely shredded cabbage in the kitchen sink only to keep my mind off it.

Just as I had broken my wooden pencil into two—in class, on purpose—agitated with the way the girls in my sister's class mocked her oily braids.

It's not explicit why I broke the porcelain doll in the master bedroom to alert my family of a visiting uncle's misdemeanour while he kept whispering—*it's okay, it'll be fine, I'm sorry, I'm going away;* and it's possible I've broken many other things, and not felt, in the least, guilty.

Today, stirring the chicken curry, Mum pours in ghee and copious amounts of grated garlic. On the side, she chops the coriander perfectly, then begins arranging the kitchen racks full of jars that came with us here—jars waiting replenishments from back home, of desiccated coconut, turmeric and tamarind, and a lot else. Lily and I take the Alsatian for a walk, and once back, we feed and bathe it so Father can boast to his friends, like a true brown Sahib, how he'd always wanted to own a big dog like *that*. And, how he'd repeat, for the n-th time, *Don't mind two daughters, we never wanted a son*. Which by now we've known, by the tone of it, and how our grandparents discuss the topic, is utterly untrue.

Afterwards, we two sisters dust the sofa, set flowers on brass vases, set the wine glasses, and do the dishes, all neat and pretty, like girls our age must be—obedient and mannered. We set the table with sweets and deep-fried appetizers before those friends of Father descend to 'party', like most Sundays, as though our home in this New Jersey suburb is a colonial clubhouse, except for the Bollywood crooner without music. It is the same, only chatter and laughs meant to outdo others.

When the fun starts, it is beyond nine, and we imagine our schoolmates in their beds flipping a book or playing a video game, while Lily and I carry plates of freshly fried snacks from the kitchen, we womanly-girls, well-brought up daughters of respected family-line. I think of the Chemistry lesson I badly need to work on, perhaps all-night, when Mum calls me again to send along a tray of her best gold-edged cups and a large pot of tea.

The skyline is melting away, swirling into blackness, and I hear Mum coughing, above the sound of flaming oil being swirled by the ladle; find Lily texting grievances to one would-be friend (only if the girls in her group really want to be called 'friends'), and that Alsatian demanding dinner. It is then I happen to overhear one of Father's acquaintances saying something in appreciation, and Father laughing loudest. I remember the dog howling when I barge into the party, amidst an excited conversation on the sudden topic of marriage and marriageable girls, and, manage to catch *Your eldest is beautiful*, quickly followed by, *I know a suitable boy. He's a doctor at Boston.*

Did I know how a tuning fork felt when slightly struck in Physics lab, or a matchstick dismissed its fate just before being lit? I knew—*then, there.*

Mum rushes in, the oily ladle still in her hand, the look of helplessness.

Amidst protests, I stay fearless and loud.

Instead of feeling sorry for something broken—unexpected, unfortunate—I feel the crackle of my words still resonating, like a cautious but urgent step on an unbroken path made of sandless silica.

Someone Like Annabelle

Let's imagine pure mechanics. Not fire. Instead of glass, let's talk attraction and repulsion. What is to be stirred with two scoops of isinglass so courses of molecules change, or solidify like glue, or say, become viscous?

Milk must be stirred, sugar added like love. Annabelle was stirred. Mum too.

The takeaway dinner from Alimuddin's Indian Kitchen lay unboxed. Outside, the wind is like Siberia visiting Alaska. Lily and I stand at the door eavesdropping on another steadily rising argument.

Father had become suspicious that evening that Mum was being unfaithful and stirred the household like never before. One more in the series of his accusations, and her denials. Just that this time, it wasn't a minor domestic issue, it was a *man*—one of Father's friends.

Many weeks went by with Father sleeping in his car most nights and doing extra shifts just so he didn't have to come home.

Lily and I try in vain to be as normal as possible. The type of normal one feels while a tiger is preying on a deer in the jungle, and a river is flooding a flat-plain back home.

We keep off schoolwork most days because we don't feel like doing them. A famous televised court trial plays one evening after school: a family that had been house-hunting, had finally zeroed in on a large house, named Tersa's Manor. They thought the name was high society, classy, the house itself large and well-built, and paid a deposit. On the final inspection they found a termite pair on the floor just above the basement. The broker quashed the pair with his shoes but the deal wasn't 'on' anymore, the buyer had gone to court saying it was as good as a house of cards.

We look at each other. Our house of cards, never very strong, was breaking down.

Father, long used to being treated as the lord of the house, randomly threw fits of rage; now he'd begun to come home only on the weekends late into the night, eating leftover food and again leaving before Mum woke up.

He comes home one morning with the mortgage papers. He had paid off the taxi-cab's loan. He wasn't telling, but we knew that was the case.

For a start, Father just dishevels the laundry Mum had just been folding.

Mum breaks down. *There's nothing, there's nothing*, she keeps sobbing. But being suspicious in a relationship cemented with trust, is really cruel, it eats away the insides like termites.

We Stay As You Left Us

Two hours to our departure, I brush-paint bogies yellow, red, with merry play people, in the coloring book from second grade I'd found when they shifted our furniture and emptied the cabinets. I let the sparkly colors trickle down my faded childhood, the train's glass windows reflecting a fiery sunshine.

The phone rings somewhere. I hear Father pick it up. Laugh. Happy laughter. Like he used to when we reached an inner corridor on imaginary rails, me at his shirt tail, the weight of our shadows on him, sometimes making a rattling noise as we passed bridges. Mum whistled, Lily and I went choo-choo-choo, steps synchronized like wings.

We stay as our childhood left us. Only, the magic has escaped in steam. Our holiday train has drawn into a sea-side station on a day battered by snow storm. Routine lives have leapt from over a moss-printed cliff, crashed below, and been stabbed by erratic sharp waves.

The bogies remain buckled, stranded on the platform.

Close as Breath

When the birds of unknown ancestry went into the air with their wings flapping, the occasional glide, Mum always asked me to look away, screamed, 'Girl!' like a warning, a siren gone off. I knew what she meant. I always knew we'd return to carve out a home in the crook of the country-house that belonged to my grandfather, in India. Yet, I marveled at the flights above—they who soared were my friends. Ones who had their freedoms, their delicate exotic formations against azure skies.

I unclip myself from the scene above, and then, sitting in the lawn chair, pour over my *Metals and Non-metals* book. Later, gazing into the void, I had hoped it wouldn't happen, prayed in silence.

Yet, it happened. *It had to.* We had flown back. Only it was much earlier than expected.

When I stood and stared at the gates of my new home, how they were not really gates, just an expanse of green paddy fields we'd plough later, at the end of which the two-storied manor-style house stood, Mum was screaming again: Girl!

Threshold-crossings have great significance in our culture. Owners step inside a new home with feasting and fanfare, the moment captured on camera to be enshrined inside a golden photo frame. The new bride walks across it, when her Mum-in-law allows her, preceded by solemn mantras and rituals. I knew my crossing over wouldn't be the same, so I waited on the other side.

"Come!" Mum lurched to take me by my arm, get me across the gates of *Eddy Villa*. She sprang back in shock, for I had no pectorals. They had long been chiseled away. I think the final plumes fell off on the flight we came by, that's where my wings would be, lying discarded in a desolate corner.

Standing there frozen, I thought of my friends from school, back in the place we'd just left, hundreds of miles between us. The scrapbooks. The multi-colored pages. The music CDs. The Britney Spears posters. The Spice Girls Slam Book. The banter. The road I cycled by. The bend with the yew tree, the parks we went to, and then, these gates.

I thought of my bestie in school, the manner of her immigrant Mum saying, *Talent skips a generation*, while scornfully looking at her. Her Mum knitted a cream-and-blue striped sweater for her brother, as though that's everything talent is called for. Minutes later, my bestie was pulled away from her homework, and summoned to make tea and samosas for a visiting neighbor. We had been looking for synonyms of 'close,' our textbooks scattered on the mat. I watched her open notebook, the blank pages fluttering like frosty-white wings, wishing to be set free to soar the sky.

'Close' is snug, tight, not being distanced in time, space, or significance. Back at the place we lived in then, my chosen synonym fell into place in the high school essay I had been writing—close was too common a word in my opinion back then.

It wasn't.

Soon enough, my bestie's chapati-rolling talent was displayed to a prospective groom's Mum. *She makes the best ones—thin, perfect discs; you'll see when she makes them in your kitchen.* Seven people had laughed in approval of the comment.

An Indian daughter is not quite 'close' to her own family.

The rest of our high school brood continued to soar, and I think that's because there were new skies to measure, many high-rises to inhabit. They were lucky to have been raised in cages with the traps left open, whether by design or by accident. I reckon they'd never return. Not even when dying, a last homecoming. Not like me who was taken to roost with ancestors, to where they lived and finally rested.

Later, I followed Mum across the gates, further, between rows of paddy, the jamun tree, and the palm and date clusters.

I became closer to strangers and strangeness.

I think I changed.

I breathed—the breath so long that I felt the whiff of air on my chest. The intimacy of the place I had grown up in, my former life, escaped in a breath's closeness, became the luxurious, synonymous word for 'longing' that wasn't even close.

Lambda

Eight years ago, the night before my parents left, I remember how Lambda reclined on his armchair, bony legs like long strokes joined at the knee. I knelt on the dew-damp terrace, frock hem skimming dirt, observing the luminous band of stars in the dark void above.

Now that we had settled into Eddy Villa and Father was happy, it was not difficult for Mum, Lily, and me to accept that this was for the best. At least Lambda would be feeling better wherever he was. I loved him. Missed his presence.

My grandpa looked like his namesake, sitting on that chair of his in the hall all day. Hence the name I called him by—*Lambda.*

He didn't mind me calling him so. When someone carried him to the terrace, like that night, he shared snippets of his life and that of the stars. I treasure-collected, knowing they'd last me a lifetime.

It was a speckled night. He spoke little: we both knew it was probably our last. It *had* been our last, he died soon after.

Pointing to the dense packed stars near Scorpio, the constellation under which I was born, he said he didn't expect to find the core of our galaxy, obscured by interstellar dust, but he knew that's where the heart of the universe was located. I squinted hard, hoping to surprise him with discovery.

The wait for his silence to end stretched longer than ever. In my mind, I scrawled notes—too many to fit into the moment, too inadequate to fill my comprehension.

Downstairs, in Eddy Villa's hollow, pillared corridors, lost sounds reverberated—of those it was meant to house: his children, their families. Rooms, balconies, halls, Venetian windows—he'd wanted them to stay as a large joint family. Jobs, partners, opportunities, tastes; they'd left one by one. We were the last.

"I bet the Wild Ducks will never find their way, Lambda!" I said, my shrill adolescent voice perforating the stillness.

"Won't let them go," he said, with a wistful glance at the spectacular open cluster close to the Sagittarius.

"Let's swim." I wanted to make this evening like usual, just the same.

"Go, go, go!"

Lambda paddled his infirm limbs as we pretended to drift, imagining ourselves remnants of a collapsing gas cloud.

It lasted only a few seconds before he was panting.

"Keep looking out. I didn't say we're done," he shouted

I flung my arms, flapped them like wings, swam some more, watching him follow me.

"Lambda, a dolphin! *Delphinus*!"

"Sure, my child!"

The words came like dimming light, truncating my final lap.

We sat in silence again. Hoping he wouldn't notice my wet cheeks, I devoured the sight of the galaxies accelerating *away* from each other. *Breaking away.*

Lambda observed his namesake, the cosmological constant, lending itself to the eternal expansion of the universe.

Carbon is a Stranded Stone

—Carbon/Charcoal—

Coal Sack is a dark nebula which comes up the path of the Milky Way galaxy, obstructs it, much like the evening before Elemelo's day of hope. The scales of balance are heavily tilted against this minor entity, left stranded between a life of too much happiness and none. Yet he thinks Jo's father will take it if he manages five grand before the wedding, two every month after that, and let his daughter live with him. Live? Then, Elemelo must rent a room. That will be another one grand, plus their expenses. He can feel a meteor shower pound his chest. The embers are floating around the charcoal oven, gulping the air he's blowing through a bamboo pipe. He can hear someone overstepping on the accelerator. The café boys are yelling, the cashier quibbling with a customer. His drawstring pouch with all his twenty months' earnings is swinging against his thigh, and the excitement of the day off tomorrow—the secret rendezvous with Jo at the hilltop tower, her face lit up in gratitude for a promise well-kept—raises his spirits. Elemelo's happiness begins to color the western sky in a riot. His bright day awaits.

Until then, gusts of wind slap the tea-stall abutting the highway. A huge grunt announces the oven is ready to warm the slightly-dented aluminum vessel for tea that the laborers have asked for.

—Stranded/Graphite—

Four hundred years after the spyglass was improvised to reveal an intricate pattern on the moon, the turtles nest on the dark patches where light is drawing a moon-mosaic on the island floor floating on Southeastern Indian Ocean. If we sailed on a ship from *Eddy Villa* near the shore, to this island, it'd take us a mere three hours. White sands and round, smooth pebbles span the narrow strip between turquoise waters and tropical forest, centuries count time with interlocking braided roots of *Padauk* and *Mahua* but can't save the speck of earth from waves that gnaw at it and nibble away tiny bits with each tide. Leaves dance in the air and fall; the turtles wobble between the firmness of land and miles and miles of brine, hatch nestlings and look to return to their rocking life in the depths. These days, however, the sunrays also etch a precariously-inclined oil-ship on the horizon. Ripples glisten with the spill. The trees know the turtles are stranded. Soon, turtles' remains will leave minute freckles of organically produced carbon, crystallized into graphite.

Until then, a gentle breeze sways the island like a baby's cradle.

—Stone/Diamond—

Five billion years since a cloud of gas and dust collapsed to form the star that scorches an empty runway, a stranded traveler observes a vulture as it swoops and lands with geometrical precision. Through the floor to ceiling glass of the terminal building, on a precise canvas of space and time, his life is hyphenated from before his week-long-visa expired and after flights were suspended indefinitely. Immobilized without recourse. Pandemic-necessitated. The orb breathes in and out, doesn't mind the traveler from Germany, frozen at the same spot, gazing into the black holes of his past—distances that'll never be breached. Forty-fifth day. The solitaire that pricks his chest through the breast pocket still smells of Heena's *itr*. At the end of the corridor is the man who mops the already shiny floor every day at this hour. That'll be two hours before someone from the Charity will be here—food-packets for souls entrapped by this massive aerodrome. Every meal, he hopes, will be his last in Heena's country, so spiteful is he of her. Every moment spent reliving the final fight they'd had, that ended with her flying eighteen-hours-around-half-the-globe to be back at her parents'. Laws of attraction made him follow her. 'Heena loves Munish', 'Munish loves Heena', he remembers the etchings they made on stones and pillars.

She made sure it was cosmic-dramatic. Flung the wedding ring to an elliptical orbit, it came rolling across the room to him. Now here he was. Alone. Fallen into a deep crevice without anyone's notice.

Until his meal arrives, he'll watch the mop-strokes paint an abstract landscape on the floor.

Stitches

There was a grandmother's bag, *Thakurmar Jhuli,* from where emerged stories, a sleeping princess, four suitors, a golden band, a silver magic wand. On our occasional visits, we girls went to sleep listening to our grandmother reading those tales. Above our sleepy heads were hand-fans, on which coasted dreamy little mushroom clouds of color, deftly painted on palmetto slates stacked and stitched together. Waved gently to bring in a whiff of breeze, they blew away, even if for a few minutes, the gigantic worries gathering over us.

When a year rolled over, I gave up my dream of an education. We toiled in the fields. In the brittleness of the caked soil in our palms, from farmlands oscillating between tidal floods and ruthless droughts, I stowed away those little dreams.

In the afternoons, I sewed to make ends meet, like the girls in the neighborhood. In tandem, we threaded our mouths shut, like the one-horned animal and fantasy floral appliques we affixed on cloth; only the sounds of the machines and eyes measuring the shadow of the decanter kept just outside the windowless room, changing size and course with the sunlight, before finally obliterating itself.

That was the time we girls rose from our treadle machines, the metal plate just above the floor stopping, stunned into silence from the force on it all day.

Stacking our days' worth of baby frocks onto the lady's table, we went to the washroom in the backyard, once a cowshed, just a mirror on the shelf above the sink.

I watched everyone's little dreams return to their bearings as the girls took turns in front of the mirror. Dusk-light tinged their faces as they wore make-up for secret escapades with connoisseurs of their dreams, away from prying eyes of parents toiling away making a living, never to know. When the girls were finished, they looked around for approval, but I didn't dare spare the thoughts that honestly whirled in my head (they either looked too old for their years, or too juvenile in their efforts); instead, I nodded, applauded. Their endeavor, I was sure, was just a staircase to their dreams taking shape in places where the boys worked and from where they came to hunt for brides.

We emerged, always to the lady's perplexed face, and without acknowledging the payments she made to us on per-day-basis with as little as a nod, we marched out to where our rickety cycles stood in perfect columns, and pedaled towards destinations of our choices.

Mine wouldn't be too distant—a right turn towards the erstwhile colonial cemetery, and then cycling by the high red-brick walls of the ramshackle rice-mill, and then the narrow lane home to Eddy Villa.

Though times were difficult, every next day the girls fanned dreams like a hand-fan over the slow embers of an earthen burner. The sew-girls stitched together elegant but sturdy plumes on their delicate limbs meaning one day to fly. Thought of fledglings—inspired not to stop trying even if some plummeted to the ground.

At nights, on the terrace of a quiet house, I viewed the winking stars in a galaxy ever-expanding with possibilities, carrying little bits of giants. I thought of sew-girls who had been plucked off the firmament, girls who had found dreamless, sleepless nights in lover's arms. Remembered those who had eloped, but had returned from marital homes piled in nightmares. One of the girls had chosen to truncate her life—hers was a dream too distorted to last ever after.

The terrace seemed to unfurl a glittery veil above my head. Stitched together was an array of stars on a fabric of black, an applique of a golden moon. I amused myself imagining a tiara for a princess-in-waiting with the sprinkling of silvery meteor shower that happened past midnight.

In the new mornings, and on Sunday afternoons, upon the sunset-hued beach nearby, I went cycling.

When I pedaled, I felt light and fluffy as a bird, on wings of dreams, like the sew-girls.

The wheels kept turning, marking a neatly-penciled line, drawing courses of lives.

Tide

We marvel at the hypocrisy of the waves gnawing away at our barely-standing modest dwelling but never quite gobbling it. Lily and I sit on the floor by the broken table, the corners of which are encroached by drifted sand, and watch a dinghy being cradled. We keep an eye on the road between the port and the city. Mum would be here any moment, and we can't believe so will be Dan, one more time.

Monsoon clouds are closing in: we'll be ambushed again. I draw the awning of our tiny store, carved out of this home by razing a wall; stocking everything a traveler may need—knick-knacks, salted-peanuts, tobacco—because there's not another one in miles. Across the marsh, a rickety blue bus swaying like a drunken elephant makes a stop. Minutes later, Mum drags Dan in by the elbow like an errant schoolboy. Mum's face is lit up by the innocence of abandon. So is Dan's, who is adequately impressed having Mum waiting for him at the bus-stop. He ruffles his hair, styled like a *mofussil* actor; wears over-sized goggles that slide on his bony face, and ignores us as he enters, though we're at sniffing distance.

Dan throws his rucksack on the bed and lights up. We want to vanish but our rented home is only one-roomed, we can distance ourselves only so much. Lily begins to arrange Father's books one more time and I wash the dishes. We hear him ask about the goats we're rearing, and what there's for dinner. She tells him about the wave that expunged part of our backyard last week, her aching neck. I can't hear as much as a sigh.

The rice-steamer begins to rattle but it can't drown out Dan's boisterous bragging about his life in Mumbai. We doubt every word, think Mum's distant cousin only visits her when he needs to escape the law. We've spied on him on previous occasions, discovered watches and gizmos in his rucksack, currency peeping from his socks, but Mum chooses to be oblivious, stuffing his palms with scrapings from our meager cashbox every time he leaves.

For a week after he's gone, we go hungry; there's no money but Mum stays in that dream, smiling to herself, before descending into delusions and rambles. She keeps screaming about the tide that had entered our family paddy-fields five years ago, turned the soil saline, uncultivable. The tide had forced us to sell Eddy Villa, eaten our Father, because Father had poisoned himself unable to bear the strain.

As much as we try, we can't stop her from piercing her forearm with crotchet-needle until it resembles a minefield, or her emotions to explode in a tirade against us who outlived Father.

Gusts of strong winds beat down the windows, heralding another tropical storm. Dan fishes out a smartphone from his hip-pocket and begins to click Mum, she ripens, thrusts her breasts at the lens. He joins her, holds the camera so he can capture a moment of orchestrated intimacy, brings his lips down.

We relegate ourselves, wish we melted into our whitewashed walls.

Running down the stone steps, we can still hear them. We escape, barefoot, over the jutting concrete remnants of the sea-wall that once ensconced this house and into the wrath of the elements, but feel relieved.

The sea wasn't here last month and was still farther the months before. It has encroached upon our home, subsumed us a little more today, like Dan.

Over the salting, behind the casuarinas on our right, it is already drizzling. We descend into the brine, let the baby-waves nibble at our feet. They aren't that bad after all—they caress and giggle, dissipate into swarming bubbles that drown out the simmering pangs within.

Lily stretches out her arms begging to be hugged.

Winds slap at our faces with a generous sprinkling of warmth and salt. The black clouds close in. We hold our breaths, wait for a loving embrace.

A Harvest Mismatch

Harvest is time tracking, simple as flicking a switch

"Peel them!" Mum will be stern. Girl will ignore Mum, fiddle with the pleats of her gorgeous kanjivaram saree, check her braid, pull her jasmine *gajra* from the back to the front, let it cascade over her ample breasts.

The double-storey manor-style house, *Eddy Villa,* that Mum and Dad bought from the peasant family, is decorated with pretty flowers today. The flurry of activity must be offensively pronounced—no one for miles should miss that this house will host a wedding soon.

Mangoes are generally harvested at a physiologically mature stage and ripened for optimum quality

Boy will look at her overripe-ness, glance at *his* simple parents, *her* over-eager parents, saffron-hued *Alphonso* arranged in a pretty cane basket, sweetmeats of nameless hues, snacks dripping oil. He'll evaluate vintage of the silverware on the teapoy.

Girl will arch towards the basket, pick the plumpest of the fruits. Curl fingers around its softness. Imagine a hardness.

Boy will notice her, think of juices. She'll happen to measure his chances, and smile rather awkwardly, before fumbling to return the fruit to the basket, everything to order.

Fruits are handpicked or plucked with a harvester.

Girl and Boy will listen to conversations about wedding dates, arrangements, invitations.

Mum will begin to strip the fruits—jelly-like, luxurious. Offer the prospective groom a slice.

She'll be a tad upset—fruits are leaking.

"Jo!" she'll shout in anger, for no apparent reason.

Girl knows it's only Mum's concealed rage in thick pulpy flesh. Mum is privy to things even Dad isn't. He'll never approve of the web she's spinning in the boughs in their backyard, under the heavy, green canopy.

To harvest your mangoes, give the fruit a tug. If the stem doesn't snap off easily, it's raw.

The seed is small and thin and the firm flesh is crisp. The flavor is sharply sour and can be slightly bitter due to concentrations of oxalic, citric, and other types of acids.

Girl will gather the peels, recede to the kitchen, remain there until Boy Groom is gone, still fiddling with her gajra and looking out the window that opens into the yard. She'll be humming a soft tune, thinking of a brief encounter that would have happened hours ago under the cluster of mango trees had this stranger family not been here.

Mango is an ancient fruit, as old as 4000 years.

After Boy leaves, she'll place the basket of produce center-stage on the kitchen counter, tiptoe out. Under the warm summer sun, someone will call out in a low, boyish, mischievous voice, "Jo! Jo!" short for Jyotsna meaning a moon-y night, clear as crystal glass. Elemelo will be careful to let the breeze carry the name through the vines and boughs and trees in the yard. In a minute's time, Jo and Elemelo will be together. She'll wrap her arms around the boy she's in love with and will squash him to *chutney*.

Rodent Behavior

Different standardized behavior patterns exist in the natural world—ants, bees, worms—according to the other girls, according to the we-know-all women around, but for best results, *they* say, familiarize yourself with the species, and methodology, before committing to studying it.

She scribbles vigorously until lab class is over. Preserved specimens line the walls: reptiles swimming in formaldehyde, frozen eyeballs boring into her.

Afterwards, discharging puke into the dormitory sink, she retraces her steps to the concrete school building—humongous and intimidating—holding untold histories and secrets in its piers and lofts.

Later today, the cleaner boys will be there, beyond the boundary walls, subscribing to daily order. Trucks parked on heaps of rubble, ready to unload trash. They'll squabble among themselves, but gawk at her when she arrives.

At dawn again they'll vanish into clouds of dust.

Sometime tonight she'll deviate from the behavior pattern expected of her.

Of course, this Missionary Boarding School is a utopian afterthought, array of misfits she doesn't try to fit into; classes, distraction from her meaningless expressions, impaired focus, ill-at-ease limbs.

When she walks to the teacher's desk, past rickety student desks, and the putrid smell hanging in the room because of unwashed uniforms and that bin right outside the window, the class boys whistle, low and audible only to her—they can smell what the girls can't.

She ignores them—menace. Pests.

Unloading the fire-ants she's carried in her pocket back from the field between the two buildings into the desk in front of her, she sits back. Squeaks, when students in rows ahead of her squirm.

Scrap of paper teacher has just given her, is crumpled in her hand, a trophy for the newest inmate. Mice must get into the tub, swim across, act handsomely. If they're found to generate preconceived outcomes, they win twelve-digit-identifier-string that says—

Outlier. Permitted.

She's Venus beyond the precincts of the Missionary Home. Scales barbed wire fencing easily, timing her escape perfectly to guards hallucinating in opium-induced hibernation.

At six weeks pregnant, she can still very well manage to be queen with the cleaner boys. Unleash the power that nature has given her.

Later, she lets the ink swallow her, powder her to grit.

Tomorrow the guards wouldn't be too surprised to find one more girl missing. They would not be too perturbed about emergency medications shoved behind the antique cabinet in the hallway, or about a girl whose name wouldn't be easy to recall. They'd wonder if it was the girl who, they'd heard in random gossips, had run away from her family after the father died and the mother was having an illicit affair. Has a habit of running away.

Was the name *Lily?* They'll ask each other in a tone which magnified that this girl was unworthy of sympathy.

The mice will scatter in the commotion.

Some of them will regroup again in the shadow of the damp wall.

Porcellanidae

In these parts, the mice have fun while the crab-girls wear skirts a little above their knees, twist their arms to look like unfurled bright petals. They glaze porcelain bodies to resemble a floret blooming. Or a trap.

At times, they fall into these traps themselves.

Jo knows these things.

Yet, Jo wants to be a crab-girl. Like the crab-girls, she wants to race bicycles with boys who are not brothers. For a laugh, write secrets on blackboards for the class to see, and when everyone rolls their eyes, she fancies the thrill of notoriety.

In the torrent of monsoons, Jo sees the crab-girls make a chain holding onto each other to scale the grey, slippery tide walls. *Come down, behave*—their Mums shout, words they ignore with a subtle nod to each other. Once on top, they pose under the hee-haw raindrops as little czarinas while the town changes to something else. The marble hills become tree stumps; their schoolhouse, some imaginative kid's sandcastle. Their little sisters become skipping puppets, and the sparrows that romp on the spill of muddied paths become bees with golden helmets, and the truant boys from their class? Oh, Jo fails to imagine. Mongrels?

When the estuaries get flooded, and the surge rises furious, threatens to swallow their homes, they get rid of their crab-shells, swim back to sea, defiant on the saline waters, never looking back, and then away, away, away, following the rules of flowing water.

When their times will pass, which is in every crab-girl's life, and if they survive, someone will see them claw their way back, like an act of divination, back to being regular, obedient girls.

Ah! They've come back! They're back! The people will cheer them aloud.

The crab-girls will be more delicate now—Jo knows that. Compacted, flattened bodies, adapted to living and hiding under rocks on the sea bed. They'll listen to strangers chanting and tossing opinions like alms; neither nod nor answer back.

Jo knows these too: the new crab-women who have shed their limbs to escape predators.

On moon nights, when the tides beckon, they, like little wilted weird flowers, will stay harmless, on the soft, slushy path that once led to their freedoms.

On the Sunday Before He leaves, Lily is the Lighthouse

If she paid singular attention, he would seize the fiery star, pluck the traversing globules, and lead them to new lives.

Lily listens to Munish, smiles to show it. Between them are lustful waves, all these licking lies. Nothing squandered, little gained. Deliberate. Profound.

On another planet, Munish smokes Havana, visits his weird friends, old lovers, and his Mum's home, but never Heena's. *I never knew Heena*, he tells himself often. As though to convince an inner being.

Ghosts of his avatars spy on what is his swinging life. Lily thinks they relish getting to know her—a woman who ran away, eloped, birthed a stillborn. Sky beneath her feet is fallow land.

Munish punctuates the tune he is humming to ask: *Who sticks those pretty sequins upon the veil you wear?* He surveys the blackness above and kisses Lily. Her islands are a cratered world he never notices. Results of violent collisions, impact mountains thrown up on the opposite side, as rebound, as forces of nature. Ancient mariners who arrived at the broad bluff, shuddered at the ugly evil dermis, damaged, hurt in many places. Then, they put up a lighthouse, loved it like nostalgia.

He's not the one she expects an apology from. Instead, when Munish tries hard to banish those things off her thoughts, she joins him to look at the stars.

Lily thinks of herself as the lighthouse. Waits. Waves him a beam whenever he chooses to come. Like the other Sundays before this. Embraces him when he drops anchor. Learns to substitute the lofty masts for pristine promises.

She tricks herself to believe his tales. On the verge of a lover's deck, she surrenders.

Together they watch hulls and sails and steam leaving smokestacks. Watch another bunch of merry people descend on the sands.

Later, they catch more of those daring sailor boys dragging their girls up the spiraling staircase, the girl's scarf in hand, laughing and talking, and when on top, under ceaseless stars, they'll tell the girl: *I will seize the fiery star, pluck the traversing globules...*

All those sequined stars wink and look away.

Easy as lies, receding like waves, nothing stays forever on a Sunday like this.

Jamun

Sometimes, as a naïve five-year-old, I waited for the jamuns to ripen on the orchard next to Eddy Villa. Picked them up when they fell to the ground. Overripe, thick purple fleshy, tasting weird, took them to Mum.

Sometimes, older, I plucked them off the cluster—raw, green and hard. Just for myself.

Sometimes I imagined myself as the tree: glossy dark leaves, boughs too dark for anyone to conquer. Hollows, cradle for mythical nurseries to form.

Sometimes, as an adolescent, I spent breezy afternoons curled on a branch: so tranquil—like proxies for the eons no one's ever counted.

Now I stand under the Jamun tree like a forever child, lonely. The jamuns that satiated once are too high, too distant; they only stain my days, a distinct purplish patch.

Introductory Flying Lesson

1. *If you spent 30 minutes in the air on a small plane, you'd wish to be reborn as a bird.*

    This was his reply when I asked him if the plane was a Cirrus Aircraft. The man-boy in a smart uniform, someone so different from boys I'd seen in these parts. He ventured to say it was in fact the cirrus SR22 equipped with an emergency Parachute System, which can lower the entire aircraft to the ground in a relatively gentle manner. Half an hour earlier, he had had to make an emergency landing in the nearby fields, and I happened to be cycling home from work.

2. *If the fighter jets didn't make at least one flight a day, some of the parts may need immediate replacement.*

    I'd laughed. This is extraordinary!

3. *Take the controls. Taxiing. Landing.*

    If he could find the time, he promised to teach me to fly. How to read all the blinking screens, how to work the switches and tools.

I imagined him *in control.* In control of more than just the aircraft.

4. *Your flying lesson starts with a pre-flight briefing from your qualified instructor.*

    Which is me, he had winked several days later when we had met. I had nervously smiled. He'd continued, *This will cover safety, and an introduction to some of the controls.*
    Though brief, the next meeting had been special. I had revealed my love for flying, and he had shared how I could enroll for a preliminary training. By that evening, I was already dreaming. It felt as if I was inside the cockpit, *there,* the controls and lights blinking in front of me.

5. *Once in the plane, you are given headphones so that you can hear conversations between your instructor and air traffic control. The instructor and trainee will also be able to communicate with each other so you can be guided through your first lesson. Once in the air, the trainee will be able to take the controls but the instructor piloting the aircraft will take over to land the plane at the airfield and taxi back.*

    Our fourth meeting had been the longest, and before we climbed into the plane, sat in tandem, I in front, and Shavar behind me, we kissed like it was the most natural, expected thing to do.

6. *Thirty minutes in the air counts as a commendable flying time. It's an initiation.*

The initiation of our first few meetings blossomed into something deeper. Over weeks and months, we became friends then lovers. He told me about his flight sorties, why he's still a trainee pilot in the Air Force. About the compulsory ground duties before he can get commissioned, and how he loves the uniform. Shavar said he was fascinated by these smaller aircrafts but he had dreams of flying fighter planes one day.

At *thirty minus two* in the air, he told me my training was on course to my private pilot's license. And the next minute: *Let's get married*. When he said this he was the most serious I'd ever seen him, only to break into a beaming smile, plus a tight hug.

7. *Flying is cognate to fleeing. Fleeing is adventure.*

One thing was for sure: our meetings promised to be an adventure, true to the introduction to flying he'd said it'd be, and were nothing short of extraordinary

Churchyard Kurseong

There was a man dwelt by a churchyard. His wife was the enormous yew tree that shielded him from all. His children came by as autumn leaves, or as some say, they were the cattle that died grazing upon the yew. Sometimes the man coughed so hard, he'd want to be taken out to sea. But they'd trick him—his wife and his cattle-children—saying, *the season's changed and Christmas is here,* when nothing ever changed at all. So he'd stay, alone and despondent, because the churchyard's haunted—everyone knows *that*. The man married again. Then again. All the widows of British soldiers. Women who begged, sitting on the pews, who cried upon the man's shoulders, for he was a man who couldn't see them suffer. They all became yew trees on which hung tiny, ridiculous stuff—a hat, a veil, sometimes a ballerina.

At nights, the churchyard would be a little merrier, with the souls rising and hanging about, the new yews by the man's side. There would be thrill and drama, the odd prank upon the man growing terribly old. They'll still say, in the end, *This isn't Christmas enough!*

What a story! I must have laughed really loud, and only realized so when I felt someone tug my sweater.

Shavar and I looked at each other, though no one talked.

"The fainthearted should certainly avoid the place, which lies between the Dow Hill Road and the Darjeeling Forest office." The man driving the bus wasn't lying after all.

The breeze was charming, the sleepy hillock on the other side just concealed by fog. We smiled, like, telling each other it hadn't happened. For the time being we managed to shrug it off.

We walked by what we'd heard was the Death Road. The 140-year-old Victoria Boy's School, adjacent to the churchyard, was closed for the winter vacations.

We'd need to hurry; this was a haunted place. Shavar's home was a two-hour drive away from Kurseong in Darjeeling. The stopover wasn't going well.

This time, I could swear, there were sounds.

"Do me a favor," the first wife whispered in my ear, as though letting me in on a family secret. "All of us want a happy place, all his new wives and I. Take the churchyard out. Ah! If only we had real fun, with kids running about!"

I'd have sure asked people to come in and not be fearful, re-imagined a fair, for the request was earnest enough.

Shavar clutched my hand, and looked at the yew tree, and I was sure he'd been told the same thing.

Soon we saw a horse skull atop a pole, dressed like Mary Lwyd, the way they do in Glamorgan. I saw the man's legs, bony, jumping about; trailing him was the party of twenty yew trees; they were following Shavar and me!

Never be telling this to anyone, but they sang and went up the bend while we slid under a boulder and let them pass without intruding. Crouched under, and with our eyes about to pop out, we saw the parade move up the road, and, following Mary Lwyd, request admittance at the red-bricked tea-house.

That night, I remember Shavar's neighbors, those very friendly folks stopping us at the driveway to tell us that they had some lovely guests who feasted on food and ale. "It's Christmas ye' all," they said.

A German Reunion

Frankfurt Christmas market stretches from Hauptwache to the riverbank. It's a large territory to chase somebody. Heena suspected the man at the lebkuchen stand was someone she knew. Knew well.

They were neighbors in London many years ago. He was two years senior, as introverted as her. Their immigrant parents politely turned down each other's Christmas invitation for years. Till it was evident they'd soon be relations.

Heena used to peep into their yard. More so at Christmas. Ah! Music, friends, aromas. Always caught him stealing shy glances at her.

The engagement. The marriage, where everyone was cold. Both sides. Really uncomfortable with each other. The bride and groom had tried in vain to engage them in friendly conversations.

Heena felt sorry at this moment that she couldn't take the pressure anymore. Her parents had moved back to India by then. She'd taken a flight home to Secunderabad after a really bad fight.

Heena felt crushed she had turned Munish away that day, flung her wedding ring galaxies away.

Now she found herself here for work. In Germany. Where she knew he once worked too. Could it be...

Not in touch, even over phone, for two years, but she still wasn't up to the effort of quietening her throbbing heart.

Munish!

Heena suddenly realized she had lost Munish in the crowd.

With growing darkness, everything seemed smudgy and unclear around the place.

In front of her, was a beautiful recreation of the Nativity scene. A stall next to her was selling traditional brimmed hats and other pretty decorations.

Someone tapped her from behind just when Heena had given up. All lights at the Square lit up at once as the lovers hugged and cried inconsolably.

Unknot

Lily had come a long way since climbing a truck and escaping.

It wasn't the tides anymore, nor the Missionary Home. It wasn't the baby she lost. It wasn't Munish's promises she knew were not meant to last.

It was the whole.

She was at a new city. A place so different it didn't even remind her of Mum.

Tonight, she ties a knot she can unravel. One never knows—it could be like Friday last.

Carefully lowers the rope down to where the bristled edges of headlights trail each other, sedans scamper off on a rain-soaked night to warm wives and warmer dinners.

Minutes ago she had rolled away from the man. Laughed.

Envy? she had asked.

Apathy, he had answered.

She had shut out his snores, his peace bought with exertion and that snide remark, pulled the door like forever ended there.

She can still hear the shuffling downstairs, steady stream of sweating men with rounded bellies, well past midnight. But this corridor, extending up to the ghost tree, is dark and silent, the girls in strangers' arms, caged in their prisons of illusions with wrong numbers and misleading addresses. And endless promises.

Lily checks the knot's tenacity against the iron grille. The balcony railing is carved with metal peonies and doves, belonging at some time to a feudal lord who caned serfs while women waited here for his attention. Those women, she's sure, were rewarded with other servitudes.

The knot was discovered on her last attempt at escape. She had ducked in the shadows of the ghost-tree. Heard an owl hoot, bats take flight. It was like she was a marked girl. When the tides had gobbled their rented home, they'd taken shelter under polythene tents by the National Highway, hunted squirrels and bats to eat. She knows what 'game marking' is, knows how it's done.

Lily? someone calls from the stairs.

She climbs the railing, passes over each leg noiselessly, and with a little discomfort, stands on the sunshade of the window below, hidden from view, holding the rope with one hand, the other hand wrapped tightly around the grille.

She dangles one foot, like a barbed hook. Lets it lick the sins of a horrendous world busy on shame-street underneath.

Lily!

She attempts sliding lower when the fabric of her dress is caught-up in a nail protruding from the damp wall, tearing it right up to the navel, revealing the tattoo of banded-krait Dockley made for free, and of course, which Lamchan thinks is a betrayal of their relationship, as if he truly intended to own your skin. She! She who has seen promises crumble more often than the white-plaster in that window-less room.

Lily must leap. Now.

With blurry eyes, she sees the last of the red taillights bleed on the tar, vanish in the distance.

Lily? Voice of the girl from the next room. Her head is just above Lily's as she bends over, half her body folded over the railing, hand extended, face contorted, confused.

Holding the rope taut against the neck, Lily moves it back and forth like a chainsaw, and gnashes her teeth.

Coming!

The word she snaps back thrashes about the walls, self-destructs in a thousand different pixels.

Half-kissed Girlfriend

The fruits in the basket appear as though remnants of colorful, pastel-painted bogies washed ashore. Orange segments are hollow, sun-weathered cliffs. The morning nothing but washed laundry. Sounds of birds, staccato or cacophony.

I loosen the segments, arrange in a green porcelain plate, like the ones Mum stashed in her crockery cabinet. Take the plate to him. Shavar loves color. Orange against green is something he'll notice, have an appetite for. Somedays, he's fussier than a kid.

When I hold the plate to him, he picks one, licks it.

"Orange, Shavar!"

"Is it?"

I show him the peels.

"Oh, I thought," —he pauses— "lime."

On the best of days, I lose my patience. Feel guilty for hours. For patience is my armor against our fortunes, my sail against the wind.

After Lily went away, leaving a note in a long flowy handwriting, and Mother went to the weekly market to buy a set of rings and charms for Dan and never returned, and the cops said she was 'presumed' dead, I knew my wait would be longer than a lifetime. As varied as glass bangles, the intervals of time refracted like a prism.

Today is different, I can feel it. Like the sweat beads on my forehead, my patience is holding albeit with suggested impermanence.

On the last day before he'd complete the mandatory flying hours, a freak accident on ground caused a fracture on his femur and severe blunt trauma. Shavar worried he may be forced out of service. The recovery period stretched longer than initially diagnosed. Nevertheless, he was adamant he'd return to serve the country.

I had moved in with him, up north, in Darjeeling, to nurse and care for him.

Looking through a stained glass window into our intimate moments, and banishing the thoughts, I inch closer to drape a shawl over his shoulder. North wind blades through the pines, annexes the verandah. The hanging pots sway, petals fly off the flowers, hold themselves in beauty for the moments it takes to land.

"I'll get myself some coffee."

Shavar nods. Takes another orange segment, as though precious, gently brings it to his lips, keeping eyes fixated on a lonely Himalayan bulbul pirouetting on the dew-bejeweled lawn outside.

Inside, I unload the rush of tears in the sink, leave the tap running to drown out my sobs.

I fiddle with the cup, not sure if I should tell him.

"Amaira?"

I lunge and stand at the door from where I can see him.

"Amaira!"

His voice is a hiss, crawling out of the woods.

"Coming."

I know by his look. Push the wheelchair to the bathroom. I retreat to the hallway; lean on the cabinet and wait.

"Amaira! Amaira!"

I get to Shavar, wheel him out again to the verandah.

His eyes keep studying my face, convinced something is miserably awry. Trying to revive some of his lost memories from the spinal injury, I hold both his hands in mine. They are cold. I rub them vigorously, rub in heat and passion, instill desire.

He kisses the top of my palms, lingering his look on my ring-finger. I know what he wants to set right.

I kiss him on cheeks that are frigid, though my lips sear, my heart burns.

I pick the phone lying on the table, type a quick message, call the cab so I can get some groceries before nightfall.

Following Shavar's eyes, I discover the bulbul on the lawn has flown to the nearest pine branch to join its mate. Their song is a beautiful four-piece whistle, like accelerated jubilation for finding love.

Friday. Seventeen. April. It'd only been six months we were engaged. A year since his full recovery.

Shavar took the controls of his fighter jet at half-past eight in the morning. Slight rainfall, otherwise perfect conditions. Sky—the color of isinglass.

The call came mid-afternoon, when I was scraping the last of the mix into tiny molds, wiping the borosil bowls in preparation for a meal together when he'd visit, while mindful of the minutes as the auto-timer had been set.

I remember the oven hot, but not hotter than my eyes.

Prosody of Rains

Was it, *Wait for me?*

Consider his words on the last phone call. Remember the intonation, the way his voice quivered. *His.*

Row away from the island where the military truck stopped just *for you.*

Evaluate the universe around. The glassed sky still melting away, wringing itself dry in trains of raindrops, falling on the cluster of islands, over a land where the deltaic waters and sky remain smudged, coupled eternally.

There! Raindrops falling on the place where you met me for the first time—the greenery in the cashew-nut orchard, places where we were undiscoverable.

Pause. Breathe. Close your eyes. Open again.

Use the oars to lash the waves, beat them down until home. Why it had to be the last time he and you talked, why it had to be those three words on the last call, miles between you. No love words spoken; no sentiments churned. Except, longing.

Find the whiplashed tide return to slap your tiny wooden boat. Is it angry too?

Curse it! You need to hurry home, because you want to rain too, in the room where your music still lingers.

Hear the clouds grumble, spit out a lightning on the grey hill beyond the smudged grassy bank. Why do the clouds spare me?

Gaze at the archipelago around, like it were the pores of a humungous indigo skin. Pass the tiny island where the market still spills with cheap wares people buy. Not you fancying something anymore, though—glass bangles and silk scarves and colored beads mean nothing today. Ceased to have any merit long ago.

Except the one you're wearing now. Think of how he turned the silver bracelet on your wrist, how he counted for each day he was away. Then he stopped doing it because there were too many to count, like the tidal floods here. And that was after he enlisted, after he went away.

Stop. Stop right there. Stop the flow, stun the flights. Halt in the middle of the waters.

Stranded? Nay, *you* are frozen; because you just remembered the saying, *Melodic lines are in bass and treble.*

Don't mind the floodgates of memories that open, ignore the torrent bursting from your eyes.

Breathe. Tremble.

Notice the boat sway you, rock you like a baby.

Look up one last time to see the military truck pulling away with his body in a coffin, wrapped in the tricolor flag, hazy on the horizon, on the road snaking, meandering, moving farther and farther away, skirting the negligible islands.

Cullet

1. *Glass bottles and jars are infinitely recyclable*

    You shun the things that can't recycle. Father, Mum, Lily and Shavar. Moments. Time. The dead. The dozen or so times you made love. And afterwards made sweet tea with dollops of condensed milk because he loved it so much.

2. *To be recycled, glass waste needs to be purified and cleaned of contamination*

    You are ready for it. Each day is a process at that. Each day you're drifting away from what you were. You wipe table-tops and shelves, rearrange Father's books, but there's a layer of dust again, and in the evenings, out of spite, you unfasten the window facing the sea, invite the southern breeze in with a fresh consignment of sand.

3. *Recycled glass in manufacturing conserves raw materials and reduces energy because the chemical energy required to melt the raw materials has already been expended*

    Sometimes you write letters to yourself, shove them in the darkest corner of the cabinet, let the mice chew on them. Letters to Annabelle, letters to Lily, letters to the anonymous boy shivering in his undies. You wonder why it's never to Father or Mum. Not to Shavar either. Do you have nothing to say to them?

4. *Glass onto glass, the sterling effect...*

You've shattered mirrors to see if there are more of you, but in a thousand sharp fragments, it's still only you. Lonely.

5. *The life of glass is a loop-like closed circularity*

You never doubted it.

At nights, you walk in circles, the darkness doesn't make you trip and fall, the loops are infinite. Curling into embraces.

Do You Know About The Funny Parcel That Got Returned

It was for the Roye's, for their daughter's wedding, possibly a nice little present from the girl's brother who worked abroad, some construction job in Dubai or some engagement loading trucks in Mumbai or Jaipur, that brown packet the slightly forgetful postman hurled across their fence gate though it was properly locked, and their puppy tore the outer covering so it looked like an old man's wig, kicked the parcel, teeth marks all over like a battered rag doll, kicked it back so hard it landed on the cobbled lane that's artfully stained with aunt's betel spits, but of course, it was raining, and aunt wasn't out strolling and picking conversations, like: *Haan bhaiya, Mausi dikhi nahi?* to a man using a neem twig to clean teeth, enquiring about some random woman who wasn't around minding blissfully grazing goats, instead she called me when I was cycling past her window to say she suspected something, *Kuch to maamla hai!* for the Roye's were gone rather hastily, the yellow-bulbs and garage lights still on, the faucet left running, rumored gone to the groom's to pacify them for they had called the wedding off, without warning or salutation, some issue or the other, likely they were peeved at the girl's dark skin, or tapering eyes or blunt hippo nose or breasts like unripe guavas, too small and tough, or it could be about how scandalous they felt when gossip reached them that the ugly-little-harmless daughter Jo was once caught with her tongue inside this boy's mouth, what's the name? *Elemelo it is,* this popular-gossipy-neighborhood aunt casually remembers, *them together for one whole spring morning under the juicy-fleshy-mango-laden bough,* the most glittering moment in this hamlet's negligible common history aunt reckons, and how she was caned, her wings clipped suitably, and how the boy was shunted out and away to remain huddled in the shanties by the train tracks, and I strained to hear over the loud thunder claps, hoping to shut her up if she let me, so I could forage the skies wearing purple, gather some enduring comfort, or question their sneer and snarl concealed in the crowded head of tumbling clouds, or just plain be numb, while the parcel lay there, a trampled heart lying bare to sharp fire arrows, like a hammer wielding Viking beating down a soggy, sappy bundle.

Gift

The stray follows the man who picks plastic from the beach every morning. I watch while I pack meagre belongings into cardboard boxes in preparation to shift out of this rented place that now has begun to nibble at me. Mother hasn't been found.

The stray is not looking at the man, merely tracing the footmarks he leaves, like it knows them, shaped like eight, blurring away towards the tiny toe. The stray and the man stop and start, a pattern like a question, sometimes answered, often not.

The man stoops where tiny red crabs are rearing heads, cowering back, like a children's game. He picks a shell, two, then more, like the ones we girls used to thread together to wear around our necks. He puts them in his breast pocket remembering something.

I imagine a daughter, waiting.

Asking To Be Married To A Dress

It's been a year since the truck with the coffin rolled on the serpentine roads. It's been a week I've rented a new home; been sharing it with a girl from Nursing College. I'm looking for better paying work, it's something I've tried for months now, almost given up. I have pleaded the labor contractor to work on the banana plantations on the slopes of the marble hills.

The tides are miles away, no longer gnawing, no more chiseling away my present and past. That's what saves me.

I sometimes chat with the woman who lives next-door, pastes little rounded discs to sun-dry into cow dung cakes on the backyard brick wall. She tells in hushed voices, she has mislaid a basket of ripened yellow bananas this morning, left it at the new neighbor's door, the equivalent of a marriage proposal, and that this unkempt man, unemployed and useless, took the basket in, took to eating with-a-vengeance, stacking the peels like a mini ragged mountain, or like the still painting at the art museum.

I have all the time for gossips like this, so I listen: that she had no intention, was merely following divine orders, or perhaps devilish schemas, she suspected sorcery or the handiwork of the dress-wallahs knowing her daughter was of marriageable age and wedding season was up but there hardly were any sales: *The zaris have been losing color,* the shopkeeper had mentioned when they'd happened to meet at the market. *How would there be any sales?* She adds, with signature contempt: *The youth loiter, no good to marry, for there* are *no jobs—not army, not clerk, not even cooks—and nah, nah, not even sweepers, and the 'foren' machines they hire with imported brooms—what a din, like gobbling more than dirt, morning and evening.*

Acting innocent and curious, I ask: *Mausi, and what does your daughter do?* to help her story to an ending. *Oh, she makes do with the dress that we bought three summers ago, holding it against the mirror, a Bindi to finish, and when she can, she'll tie a sacred thread with a pebble to the peepul, hoping to get a suitable husband in fall.*

With bulbous eyes the woman measures me hair to toe, suddenly in doubt, borderline suspicious. She spits out the coarse betelnut she'd been chewing, and remarks thus: *Ah! Everything's* now *up to chance!* she leaves.

When she's gone, I go stand at the window, the curtain modestly drawn, until it's night, the stillness of the plantation's newly-transplanted saplings around, the cows belching to interject the calm, body stiff and brittle from the exertion of toiling through the day finding weeds to uproot in someone's garden, and when this unkempt man next-door, shirtless and scratching bristly hair, turns the kerosene lamp on. I silently watch: his room glows like fire, his body like sculpted glass. I know—

Glass is a malleable liquid that can be pressed, shaped, and molded to perfection.

There's the silhouette of a water jar, and I find myself gazing at the banana peels in the corner, the irregular mound loosening, curling and falling on each other, then at his sweaty back reclining on the rope cot, chest rising slightly, and slipping to sleep, just out of reach.

In a Room — A Chandelier Aglow

Not far away from an impressive building, in an arc drawn by Opuntias and Organ Pipe cacti, oak-dotted fields of San Francisco Peninsula, matrix of quadrangles and arcades, an architect is heard explaining the landscaping of their proposed home to the attentive Stanford couple. The couple finally deciding to turn the place into a temple of learning—a university campus. Stanford University.

We watch the documentary on TV—my son and I—intently and closely. Later, I'm going to teach him *Paint* on the desktop computer. He clicks and plays with the shape tools and vibrant colors: blue, yellow, purple, draws a merry train puffing smoke.

Children of California shall be our children, the woman in the documentary said. In a reconstruction of true events, the couple's only teenaged son Leland Jr. had died of typhoid days ago.

I can almost hear voices of students wafting in the breeze, full of life. Stanford University breathed because their boy didn't. I look at my son, the same face as his father's. Someday we hope to send him there, to Stanford. For the learning I craved, never gathered. For the dream I had long-buried deep.

We hope to afford it—his father and I. We run a store that sells hand-crafted furniture and chandeliers. In the workshop behind the store, glass is blown into spheres and cylinders until they are perfect and shiny, then joined with more intricately shaped miniature arms. To make the crystals, we melt silica sand in a furnace, mix lead, and ash. The process is laborious and delicate, but worth every minute.

Sometimes Lily offers to babysit our son and comes over after her shift at the home for the elderly she works for. Like today.

Like today *feels* special. I call her before I'm to leave for the store. She says she'll be here in half-an-hour, adding, the Home is gearing up for festive cheer. I can hear the resounding laughter of the inmates in the background, clear as glass, followed by Lily's fiery impassioned shout: LOVE YOU.

Notes on Previous Publications

- ❖ Glass/Fire – *Flash Flood*
- ❖ Un-broken – *Tint*
- ❖ Close as Breath – *Pigeon Review*
- ❖ Lambda – *NFFR*
- ❖ Carbon is a Stranded Stone – *DASH*
- ❖ Stitches – *Hypertext*
- ❖ Tide – *Gasher*
- ❖ A Harvest Mismatch – *Miracle Monocle*
- ❖ Rodent Behavior – *trampset*
- ❖ Porcellanidae – *Reckon Review*
- ❖ On the Sunday Before He Leaves, Lily is the Lighthouse – *ELJ*
- ❖ Jamun – *NFFD NZ*
- ❖ Churchyard Kurseong – *Scrawl Place*
- ❖ A German Reunion – *FFF*
- ❖ Unknot – *NUNUM*
- ❖ Half-kissed Girlfriend – *Full House Literary*
- ❖ Prosody of Rains – *EllipisZine*
- ❖ Do You Know About the Funny Parcel That Got Returned – *Necessary Fiction*
- ❖ Gift – *Five Minutes Later*
- ❖ Asking to be Married to a Dress – *NFFR*

Milton Keynes UK
Ingram Content Group UK Ltd.
UKHW042107131124
451149UK00006B/688